The Little Woodman
and other stories

The
Little Woodman
and other stories

* * * * *

Mary Sherwood
and
George Shaw

Christian Focus Publications

This edition Copyright © 2003
Christian Focus Publications

ISBN 1-85792-854-7

Published by
Christian Focus Publications Ltd
Geanies House, Fearn, Tain, Ross-shire
IV20 1TW, Scotland, Great Britain.
www.christianfocus.com
email: info@christianfocus.com

Cover Illustration by Gerard Terborch
Cover design by Catherine Mackenzie

Printed and bound in Great Britain
by Cox and Wyman, Reading

Contents

The Little Woodman
and his Dog

In former times there lived, on the borders of a very wide forest, a certain woodcutter, named Roger Hardfoot, who had seven sons. I cannot tell you the names of the six elder sons; but the youngest, who was born several years after his brothers, was called William.

The woodcutter's wife died when William was very little, so the care of the boys was left to their father only. He was an industrious man, and gained a very good livelihood by cutting wood in the forest and tying it up in bundles. These he carried, on the backs of asses, to a small town at some distance; and with the money which he sold them for, he brought back such things as he had need of for himself and his family.

He made his sons also work with him, and, as they were strong lads, the elder ones soon became able to do almost as much as their father. As a result the earnings of the family were very good, and they might have been very happy, had not that one thing been lacking, without which no family can be happy. The woodcutter was so sinful as to neglect to teach his children to serve God, and this was the more wicked, as he had himself been taught the word of God by his mother when he was a little boy.

But the woodcutter neither thought of his Saviour nor of his poor mother's instructions, until God brought him to reflection by a dreadful accident. One day, while he and his sons were cutting down a tree in the forest, the tree fell upon him and he was so dreadfully hurt that he never was able to work any more. His hurt caused a disease which, by slow degrees, brought on his death. But while death was drawing on, he suffered great pain of body, and his mind was filled with many bitter thoughts; all the sins of his past life were set before him by the almighty power of God, particularly his neglect of his mother, who was a widow, and from whom he had run away many years before. And now he began to remind his sons of their duty to God, often speaking to them of their Saviour, and of the world to come.

From day to day the poor dying woodman earnestly begged his sons to turn to God; but they mocked at him and would not listen to him. He could now work for them no longer, nor provide for them what they wanted; so they followed their own business and pleasure, hardly taking care to provide their sick father with common food or clothing. One only of all his sons took pity on him and listened to his advice, and waited upon him. This was little William, his youngest child. He was just five years old at the time when the tree fell upon his father and his heart was not yet grown hard, like the hearts of his brothers.

Fathers and mothers, you should lead your children to love God while they are little, and while their hearts are tender. And you, little children, lose no time, but give yourselves up to God, before you become hard and stubborn, like William's brothers.

William was now the only comfort his poor

father had in this world. When the woodcutter lay sick upon his bed, William sat by his side and watched beside him and was always ready to bring him everything that he wanted. And when his father crept out into the forest, which he sometimes was able to do, in order to take the air, William followed him; and when he sat down, this little boy sat by him; and when he knelt to pray, little William knelt by him and prayed as well as he could.

One day, when the woodman's eldest sons were gone out to steal deer in the forest, the woodman and his little boy sat at the door of their hut; while Cæsar, little William's dog, lay down at their feet. And as they sat together the woodman talked to his little boy:

"Oh, my little child! My only comfort!" he said, "how wicked was I when your brothers were young like you, that I did not try to lead them to God! But that opportunity is past, and I can do nothing for them now. They will not listen to me; they turn against their dying father; and I deserve this treatment at their hands."

"Why do you say that you deserve it, Father?" said William.

"For many reasons, my dear boy. I was an undutiful son, and for this cause, if there were no other, I deserve to have undutiful children. My mother was a widow, and one who loved God. Her house is in this forest, but three or four long days' journey from this place. I was her only child. She brought me up with the greatest tenderness, and taught me early the word of God. But when I grew up I became a lover of pleasure more than a lover of God; I ran away from my dear mother, and have never seen or heard of her since."

"And is she alive?" said little William.

"Oh, my child! I do not know," said the woodcutter. "But whether she be alive or dead, I shall never see her again in this world. I only wish that she could know how deeply I repent of my sins; and that I have fled at length to the merits of a gracious Redeemer, as my only hope of being saved from everlasting punishment. And oh, my sons! My sons! I pray for my sons in the bitterness of my soul; for as I was formerly a wicked son, so I have since been a wicked father. I neglected to teach my children the word of God while they were little; and now they despise me, turning a deaf ear to my instructions, and hardening their hearts against my reproofs."

"But," said William, "perhaps the Lord Jesus Christ may change their hearts even now, Father. Let us pray for them."

"Yes, my child! My comfort! My delight!" said the woodcutter, "We will pray for them. Every day while I live we will pray for them. This is all I can now do for them."

So William and his father knelt together at the door of the hut, earnestly praying that God would, in his good time, change the hearts of the young men.

The woodcutter did not live long after this conversation had passed between himself and his little son. In a few days he took to his bed, from which he never rose again. William now became more attentive to him than ever; and never left him but to fetch him water, and such things as he asked for. William sat beside him, and Cæsar lay at his feet; and when the woodman was heard to lift up his voice in prayer his little boy prayed with him.

On the morning of the day on which he died he told his little boy that he trusted his prayers had been heard, and that his sins were forgiven him for his Saviour's sake. He then prayed earnestly for his elder sons; after which, kissing little William many times, he begged him to remember his Saviour in the days of his youth.

Towards evening William's brothers came in with a deer, which they had killed in the forest, and a cask of brandy which they had bought from some travellers. Making a great fire in the hut, they roasted the venison, and opened their cask of brandy. They took no notice of their poor dying father, though they could not help knowing the state he was in. However, they invited William to come and feast with them; but this kind little boy would not leave his father. He sat beside him till he grew drowsy, and then lying down by him on his bed, fell asleep.

In the morning, when he awoke, he found his father quite dead, and his brothers lying asleep in different parts of the hut. So, kissing his poor father, he sat crying by him till his brothers awoke.

But, not to make this story too long, I must tell you that the young men buried their father, on the day after his death, in a dark corner of the forest, not far from the hut. And when they had closed up the grave, and covered it with sod, they returned to the hut, leaving William and Cæsar sitting by the grave.

After returning to the hut the young men sat down to enjoy themselves with the remainder of the venison and brandy. And they began to plot mischief against their little brother, whom they hated, because his ways were not like their ways. "We must not keep him with us," said one of them, "lest, when we kill the king's deer, he should tell of our practices."

"But we will not kill him," said another, "lest his blood should rise up against us."

"Let us take him three days' journey into the forest," said a third, "and there suddenly leave him. He will then never come back to tell tales of his brethren."

"But we must take care to tie up Cæsar in the hut," said a fourth, "or we shall find him very troublesome. There will be no getting him away from the child."

"Tomorrow," said the fifth brother, "we will set out. We will take an ass with us to carry the child; and we will go three long days' journey into the depths of the forest."

"But we must carefully conceal our purpose from the child," said the sixth, "that we may not be troubled with his cries."

So these wicked young men having settled their horrible plan, got up early the next morning, and preparing one of the strongest of their asses, they took their little brother out of his bed, and, hastily helping him to dress, set him upon the ass.

"Where are we going?" said William, who thought no evil.

"We are going," answered the elder brother, "three days' journey to hunt in the forest and you are to go with us."

"What! Hunt for the king's deer?" said William.

His brothers made no answer, but looked at each other.

Cæsar was ready to follow the ass on which his little master rode, wagging his tail, and capering about, to show that he was in a hurry to be gone; but one of the brothers came with a cord, which he fastened round the poor dog's neck, and dragged him into the hut.

"May not Cæsar go with us?" said William.

"No," said the elder brother.

"But we shall be away several days. Will you not leave him food to eat?" added William.

"Mind your own business, child," answered the brother, "we will take care of Cæsar."

So Cæsar was tied up in the hut, and all the brothers being now ready, they gave the ass a stroke with a stick, and began their journey into the forest.

They first went down a deep, dark path, where the trees were so thick that the light of heaven was almost shut out; then they began to ascend a steep hill, sometimes turning to the right and sometimes to the left.

In this way they went on, as fast as the ass could trot, continuing their journey till noon; when they stopped under a large oak tree to feed the ass, and to take some refreshment themselves, which they had brought in leather bags upon their backs.

After an hour's rest they began their journey again, and went on till evening; when they came to a cave, in a deep hollow, near which a spring of water gushed out of the rock. At the mouth of this cave the brothers lighted a fire, for fear of wild beasts, and having eaten supper, laid themselves down to sleep.

The next day they continued their journey into the depths of the forest, where they saw many deer, which peeped at them from among the undergrowth, and then ran away. At night they slept on a little circle of grass, which they found in an open part of the forest. But one of the brothers was obliged to watch all night, to keep up a large fire, which they had lighted for fear of the wolves, whom they heard all night howling and baying around them.

The next morning they began their last day's journey. The ass was much too tired; but this, however, did not disturb these hard-hearted men. They drove the poor creature forward without mercy, taking little rest, till they came, towards dusk, to a place where four ways met. Here they halted, and having lighted a fire, they sat down to eat and drink.

"We have been travelling three days," said little William. "Are we now at our journey's end?"

"Do you think we are come far enough?" said the elder brother, laughing.

"I do not know what you are come for, brother," answered William.

"To steal the king's deer," replied the young man.

"But there are deer much nearer our hut than this place; why should you come so far to steal deer?"

"You will know soon enough," was the only answer they returned.

So after they had eaten their supper they all lay down to sleep; everyone without saying his prayers, except little William, who, though he was much tired, fell upon his knees to pray. He joined his little hands, as he had been taught to do by his poor father, and called upon God, in the name of his Redeemer, to take care of him. "My father is dead," said he to himself, "and my brothers speak very roughly and unkindly to me. I have no friend in this world to care for me. O my God! Do thou take care of me, for my dear Saviour's sake."

When he finished this prayer he lay down by the ass, and was falling asleep, when he fancied he heard these words, - "I will. Be not afraid." At this he raised up his head and looked about to discover the speaker; but his brothers were all asleep about him, except the one who was watching the fire, who sat silently with his elbows upon his knees. Then the little boy thought that these words had been put into his mind by his heavenly Father; so he felt comforted, and lay down again to sleep. Now little William was very much tired, and he slept so soundly that he never heard his brothers move: for these wicked young men, in pursuance of their horrible scheme, got up before break of day, and leading away the ass, quietly departed towards their own house, leaving William in a deep sleep upon the grass.

William continued to sleep, being undisturbed, till the sun was high enough to shine upon him through the upper parts of the trees. Two jackdaws chattering in a branch above his head now awakened him, when he sat up and looked round him. The turf on which he had been sleeping was interspersed with many beautiful flowers; there was the violet, the wood-anemone, and the many-coloured vetch; and birds of various kinds were hopping about, singing and chirping among the trees. It was a lovely morning, and the leaves of the trees were scarcely moved by the gentle wind.

William at first could not remember where he was, or how he came into that place. But when he realised that his companions were gone, and that he was left quite alone, he began to cry bitterly, and to call out aloud for his brothers. His voice sounded through the wood, but no answer was returned. His brothers were already many miles away from him.

"Oh, my brothers! My cruel brothers!" said William, "did you bring me here in order to leave me in this place? On my father! My poor father! Could you now see your little boy, how grieved you would be! But you are happy. I hope you cannot see me. God can see me, and he will pity me and take care of me. If the wild beasts should eat my body, my soul will go to heaven. My Saviour will pity me. I am a little sinful boy, but my Saviour came to die for sinners."

Then little William did what all children should do in trouble; he knelt down and prayed very earnestly for God's help.

After he had done praying he thought he would try to follow his brothers; but then he remembered that, as four ways met in that place, it would be impossible for him to know which way they went. He looked to see if there were any marks of fresh footsteps in any of the roads, but could not find any. He then returned to the place where he had slept and, sitting down on the grass, began to weep bitterly. But not a word of complaint came out of his lips; only from time to time he prayed earnestly for help from heaven; and his prayers were always made in the name of the Saviour.

Sometimes it came into his mind that his brothers were only gone a-hunting, and that they would come back again in the evening; and this made him unwilling to leave the place in which they had left him.

Towards midday, being very hungry and thirsty, he began to look carefully about for any bits or scraps of bread and meat which his brothers might have left on the grass. He found some, which he ate thankfully; and in searching among the bushes he found a little spring of water, of which he drank and was refreshed.

In this way God provided him with a meal in the wilderness, where no man lived. So poor little William was very thankful, and his trust in God was made greater by this kindness.

My dear little children, when God sends you smaller blessings, be thankful for them. God loves a thankful disposition. It is a sign of a humble mind: and God loves a humble mind; for it is written in the Bible, God resisteth the proud, but he giveth grace to the humble.

And now the time of William's hardest trial came on; but his heavenly father remembered him and had provided a place of comfort for him. But you shall hear how it was.

As evening approached, the wood became more and more gloomy. The birds ceased to sing, and went to rest upon the boughs of the trees; the crickets chirped among the dry leaves; and great bats began to flit about, flapping their heavy wings among the branches above his head. Poor little William began to think how he should spend the night, and where he could be safe from the wild beasts, for he had given up all hopes of his brothers' return. He looked about for a tree into which he might climb, for he was not able to get into a very high one, being but a little boy. After some time he found one, which he managed to climb, and among the branches of which he did his best to fix himself firmly. But he feared that he could not keep himself awake all night, though he did not dare to go to sleep, lest he should fall down from the tree.

Soon after this it became dark, and the wind arose and whistled dismally through the woods. But, what was still worse than the wind, he heard the distant howling of a wolf, which made his little heart to beat: so he sat trembling from head to foot. His fear, however, had the right effect: it did not make him cry; but it urged him to pray. He prayed that his heavenly father would be with him in his trouble; and his prayer was made, as before, in the name of that Saviour to whom his father, the poor woodman, had for the last few months of his life taken such pains to lead his young heart.

The tree into which William had climbed was directly facing one of the four ways I before spoke of; and while he was praying, suddenly he noticed a light, as of a candle or fire, which seemed to be at the end of this way or path. This was a sign that some person was near, who perhaps might take pity on him. He did not wait a moment, but lifting up his heart in thankfulness to God, he came hastily down from the tree, and ran towards the place where he had seen the light. But being upon the ground, he could see the light no longer; nevertheless, remembering the direction in which it had appeared, he ran that way with all his might; for he was very afraid of wolves. The forest was full of them.

The path he had taken went over very uneven ground, leading him sometimes up hill, and sometimes down. So when he had gone on for about half a mile, and had reached the top of a slope, he saw the light again, which looked nearer and brighter than before. This comforted him greatly; and though he did not stop running, he lifted up his heart in thankfulness to heaven. He lost sight of the light, however, almost immediately, the path just leading him down into a deep valley.

As he was running down into this valley, some clouds rolled away, and he saw the moon. It was not the full moon, but the new moon, which looked like a beautiful silver crescent rising above the woods. By its cheering light he could see that a stream of water ran across the bottom of the valley; and this filled him with fear, not knowing how deep or wide the water might be, nor how he should get across it. But he still kept running on towards it, till his little feet began to ache sadly.

And here he had a most dreadful fright for, as he was running on, he heard feet padding after him, like the feet of some wild beast, and panting which he supposed to be that of a wolf. It came nearer and nearer, till at length poor little William was so terrified that he could run no longer, but fell down at his full length upon the ground, believing that the next moment he should be torn to pieces. And now the creature came close up to him, putting his head so near to William's cheek that the frightened child could feel his breath; and presently he felt the tongue of an animal, put out, as he thought, to begin to devour him. But instead of biting or hurting him, the creature began to lick him, and to utter a cry of joy, by which William knew him to be his faithful dog, Cæsar, who had broken the rope that bound him at home, and had come all the way through the forest in search of his little master.

Oh! how delighted was the little boy when he found that, instead of an enemy, it was his only earthly friend, his dear Cæsar! He soon got upon his feet, and hugged Cæsar round the neck; while the poor dog capered about to show his joy.

At last little William remembered that he was still in the wood, in a place of great danger; so he began to run forward again, and went on till he came to the water I before mentioned. There he was quite perplexed, not knowing how deep it might be; but hearing the howling of a wolf not very far distant, he stepped into the water and tried to make his way through it. But the stream suddenly bore him off his feet; and he certainly would have been drowned, had not his faithful Cæsar dragged him up, and brought him safely to the opposite side.

Little William felt his heart full of gratitude to his faithful dog, and more so to him who had sent him such a friend. But there was at present no time for delay; he shook the water from himself as well as he could, and then began to climb the further bank, followed closely by Cæsar. And now the clouds rolled over the moon again, and made it quite dark; but still William felt comforted by the presence of such a friend as Cæsar.

So they went on together, and had almost reached the top of the hill, when William saw in the dark, not far before him, two glaring eyes of some dreadful beast; and at the same time he heard a snarling noise like that of a wolf. He stood still, while Cæsar came before him and began, in his turn, to growl angrily. At length William saw the eyes move, and the wild animal springing upon Cæsar. For a few minutes there was a dreadful noise, and a horrible battle between the faithful dog and the wolf; for it was, indeed, a wolf, who was lying in wait for prey on the side of the road.

The woods sounded on all sides with the cries of the two furious animals; and little William, not willing to leave Cæsar, though unable to assist him, continued on his knees, lifting up his hands and eyes to God; for he knew very well that if the wolf overcame Cæsar, he would next fall upon him.

For a few dreadful minutes William knew not which would be the conqueror. At length the wolf ran howling away; and the next minute

Cæsar came up to his master, and pulled him by the coat as if it were to persuade him to hurry forward.

William then ran on, and Cæsar with him, till they came to the top of the hill; when, oh what a pleasant sight! They saw, not a hundred yards before them, a cottage standing in a garden: for the light from the window was so strong that they could see even the garden rails, and the little wicket gate. William sent up a shout of joy and thankfulness, and ran down the gentle slope to the gate, which he opened in a minute. And shutting it after himself and Cæsar, began to knock at the cottage door. But so great was his impatience and fear lest another wolf should come after him, that he knocked three times before an answer could be returned.

At length he heard the voice of a woman inside saying, "Who is there?"

William answered, "A poor little boy, who has been lost in the forest, and who would have been killed by a wolf if his dog had not saved him."

"Come in, then, come in," said the old woman, opening the door. "Come in, poor little fellow: you and your dog are both welcome."

When the door was open, little William saw an old woman stooping with age, dressed in a clean blue woollen gown, and having a white cap tied under her chin. And her house was as neat as herself. There was a bright fire on the hearth, the same which had given light to poor William in the forest, before which was standing an armchair, and a little three-legged table, with a Bible lying open upon it. William did not know it was a Bible at that time, but he learnt what it was afterwards. An old grey cat sat purring by the fire. There was a comfortable clean bed in one corner of the room; and there were many shelves, filled with bright pewter dishes, against the wall. "Come in, my little wandering boy," said the good old woman; "come in, you are welcome here." So she brought him and Cæsar into her cottage, and fastened the door.

The moment William saw the door shut, and found himself safe from the wolves, he fell down upon his knees, and thanked God for his safe deliverance. Then turning to Cæsar, "My dear Cæsar!" he said, "my dear Cæsar!" Twice you have saved me from death! If it had not been for you, I should now have been eaten up by wolves."

While William was kissing and thanking Cæsar, he noticed a wound in his side, which the wolf had given him, but which the faithful dog had not heeded till he had brought his little master out of danger. When William saw the wound he began to cry bitterly, begging the old woman to give him something to cure his poor dog.

"Do not cry, my little boy," said the old woman; "we can do nothing for Cæsar's wound; he will lick it well himself. But I will make him a soft bed by the fireside, and give him something to eat and drink, and it will shortly get well."

So she brought out an old sheep's skin, and laying it on one side of the fire, she pointed to Cæsar to lie down on it. Then going to her pantry, she brought him some bits of meat, and set before him a pan of water. Now the poor dog was very hungry and thirsty, for he had been without food for several days; so he ate and drank; and when he had licked his wound he fell asleep.

"And now, my little boy," said the old woman, "as you have made your dog comfortable" (for she could not get the child's attention till Cæsar had been looked after), "tell me, had you no other friend with you in the forest except this dog?"

"No," said the little boy.

"Well, then, my child, try to relax. You are now safely housed. Tomorrow you shall tell me who you are, and where you come from; but now you shall have something to eat. I must first, however, wash your poor little weary feet, and dry your clothes, and you shall then go to bed."

Little William could not help crying when the old woman spoke so kindly to him. "Why do you cry, my little boy?" said she.

"To think of God's goodness to me," answered William. "A very little while ago I expected to be torn to pieces by wild beasts, and now I am come to you, and am made so happy."

"Poor little boy," said the old woman, "if I can make you happy, you shall be happy." And she kissed his wet cheek.

Then she put some milk upon the fire, with bread broken into it; and while it was warming she took off William's wet clothes, and having washed the dust and mire from him, she wrapped him in a blanket, and laid him in her bed, hanging his clothes to dry, ready for the morning: after which she gave him the warm milk and bread, feeding him with her own hands.

"I cannot go to sleep till I have thanked God," said William, "and till I have kissed you, for you are as kind to me as my dear father was."

"And have you not a father now?" said the old woman.

"No," said William, "for he is dead. I have six brothers, but they don't love me: and after my father died, they brought me three days' journey into the forest; and last night, when I was asleep, they left me to be eaten by the wolves. But God had pity on me. He brought me to you; and now I will be your child, and love you as I did my father."

"And you shall be my child," said the old woman. "I will love you, and we will serve God together, for you ought to love God very much, seeing what he has done for you."

"My father taught me to love God before he died," answered William, "but he could not persuade my brothers to listen to him when he would have taught them about God."

Then little William told the old woman many things which had happened before his father's death; and how his father had talked to him about his life, and had repented of his sins, and died trusting in his Redeemer.

While William spoke the old woman trembled, and was obliged to sit down on the bed by which she was standing; for she began to have some suspicion that William's father was even her own son, who had run away from her many years before, and of whom she had never since received any news. For some minutes she could not speak. At length she said, "Tell me, what was your father's name?"

"Roger Hardfoot," answered William.

"Oh!" said the old woman, putting her hands together, "it is even so – Roger Hardfoot was my son! My only son! And did he die repenting of his sins, and trusting in his Saviour? Then my prayers have been heard for him. And are you his child? Are you my own little grandson? Were you sent by kind Providence to take shelter in your poor old grandmother's house, and to be the comfort of her old age?" Then she fell upon his neck, and they both wept for joy.

"Indeed, indeed," said little William, when he could speak, "this is a wonderful day! And we will thank God together. And did my brothers bring me so far that I might find my grandmother? I shall now love Cæsar more than ever, for I never should have come here if Cæsar had not helped me through the water, and fought that dreadful wolf."

Now William was very tired, and soon fell asleep; but his grandmother (whose full heart would scarcely allow her to close her eyes) spent most of the night in praise and thanksgiving. She thanked God that her son, who had caused her so many hours of sorrow, had died in faith; and that her little grandchild had been brought to her in so wonderful a manner. She also prayed that God would turn the hearts of her elder grandchildren, those wicked young men who had treated their little brother so cruelly.

William continued to live with his grandmother till he grew up to be a man, and he did everything in his power to make her happy. He took care of her goats and her fowls, and worked in her garden; and she taught him to read his Bible and to write. They took great care of Cæsar as long as he lived, and when he died William buried him in the garden.

William lived very happily with his grandmother, because she brought him up in the fear of God; and while he was little she punished him when he was naughty.

She often used to say, "I loved your father so foolishly that I never corrected him, so God corrected me. But I will love you, my little grandson, with a wiser love, and will not fail to punish you when you are naughty."

When William grew up, he thanked his grandmother for having preserved him from doing wrong. And so their days were spent working happily together; their evenings being closed with reading God's book and praying together; till, at length, the good old woman died.

At her death she left William her house, and all that she had; and he mourned for her many months. At length, finding it melancholy to live alone, he chose himself a wife, who feared God; and God blessed him with several children, whom he brought up in the way of holiness.

When William was forty years old or more, he was sitting at his door one fine evening in summer, with his wife and children about him, and his youngest daughter was reading a chapter from the old Bible which had belonged to his grandmother, when six very miserable looking men came from the way of the forest. They were pale and seemed to be worn with disease and famine. On their shoulders they carried old leather bags, which seemed to have nothing in them. They had neither shoes nor stockings; and their ragged and tattered garments hardly hung upon their backs. They came and stood before the paling of William's garden, and humbly asked for a morsel of bread.

"We are poor miserable men," they said, "and have been many days without any food but the wild nuts and fruits we could pick up in the forest; and for several nights past we have had no rest, through fear of the wolves."

"I ought to pity you," said William, "for when I was a little boy I passed a whole day, and part of a night, alone in that forest, and should have been eaten up by one of those dreadful creatures, had not my faithful dog, whose grave

is in this garden, fought for me, and saved me."
While William spoke, the men looked at each
other.

"But you seem weary and hungry," said
William; "sit down on the grass, and we will
bring you something to eat."

So William's wife ran into the house, and
prepared a large pan of broth, into which she
broke some brown bread, and gave it to one of
her sons to set before the men.

The poor half-starved and ragged strangers
received the broth with thankfulness, and ate it
greedily; after which they arose, and bowing low
before William, they asked him if he would allow
them to lodge for that night with his goats. "For,"
said they, "we have had no place of safety to
rest in for many nights, and are so spent and
worn out with watching against the wolves that
we are like men at the point of death."

"I have," said William, "a little barn, in which
I keep hay for my goats; you are welcome to
sleep in it, and we will supply you with blankets
to cover you. So sit down, and be at ease."

The men were exceedingly thankful. William
opened his gate to them, and they came into

his garden, and sitting down round him upon the green turf, he entered into conversation with them, while his wife and children went about their work.

"And where," said William, "do you come from? Where do you propose to go tomorrow? You seem to have made a long journey, and to be in a very forlorn condition; some of you also appear to be in bad health, and look like men who have suffered much."

"Sir," answered one of the men, who seemed to be the eldest, "we were woodmen, in the forest, about three days' journey from here. Some years ago, falling under the displeasure of the king, our hut was burnt, all our things were taken, and we were cast into prison. We lay many years in a loathsome dungeon, so that our health was utterly destroyed and when we were set free we were unable to work. Having no friends, we have wandered from place to place, suffering all imaginable hardships, and being often many days without food."

"I fear," answered William, "that you committed some crime by which you offended the king."

"Yes, sir," answered the oldest of the men, "we were guilty of deer-stealing. We will not deceive you. We would now live honestly, and lead better lives; but in our own neighbourhood no one will look upon us, and we cannot raise money to buy even a single hatchet to cut wood, otherwise we would follow our old trade, and try to maintain ourselves; though indeed we are now so feeble that we could do but little."

"But," said William, whose heart began to feel pity for these poor men, and to be drawn strongly towards them, "have you no relations in your own country? Are you all of one family?"

"We have no other relations," answered the old man; "but we are all brothers – children of the same parents. Our father was a woodcutter: his name was Roger Hardfoot."

"And had you not a little brother?" asked William, getting up and coming close to them.

The men looked at each other like persons in great terror, and knew not what to answer.

"I am that little brother," said William. "God preserved me from death, and brought me to this house, where I found my grandmother still living, and a parent she was indeed to me; and here I have lived in peace and abundance ever since. Be not afraid brothers; I freely forgive you, as God, I hope, will forgive me. You have done me no harm; and now that God has brought you here, I will assist and comfort you."

William's brothers could not answer him, - but they fell at his feet, shedding tears of repentance; for God had touched their hearts in their prison, and had made them aware of the great and horrible sinfulness of their lives.

William tried to raise them, but they would not be lifted up till they had received his pardon. "We never have prospered since we left you, our little brother, in the wood," they said. "Our lives have, from that day, been filled with trouble, though they were for years afterwards spent in riot, confusion, and sin."

William at length persuaded them to rise, and to feel assured that he freely forgave them, earnestly begging them to apply to God for forgiveness through his beloved Son.

The poor men were comforted by William's kindness; but whenever they looked at him, and remembered how they had treated him, they were filled with shame and sorrow.

The next day William and his sons began to build a hut close by his own cottage for his brothers; and his brothers gave all the assistance in their power to the work.

When the hut was finished, William provided them with mattresses to sleep on, and sheepskins to cover them. He gave each of them a knife, a spoon, a wooden stool, a pewter plate, and a horn drinking-cup. He gave them, also, a deal table, and several other little articles of household goods; while his wife and daughters supplied them with coarse clothing of their own spinning.

William was also so kind as to give each of them a hatchet, which enabled them to maintain themselves by woodcutting without being a heavy burden upon their brother, although he constantly supplied them with many little comforts from his own house.

But what was better than supplying their bodily wants, he took unwearied pains to lead their souls to God. He read to them every evening out of their grandmother's Bible; and it is believed that they did not hear the word of God in vain; for they became very humble, daily lamenting their sins, and died at last in hopes of being forgiven for their Saviour's sake.

William and his wife lived many years after the death of his six elder brothers, and had the pleasure of seeing their children's children growing up in the fear of God.

And now, my dear children, I would have you learn from this story to make God your friend; for such as be blessed of him shall inherit the earth; while they that be cursed of him shall be cut off (Psalm 37:22).

The Orphan Boy

There is in the north of Scotland, in a very deep valley, a little village, in which there are about ten cottages, and a small church; but the minister does not live in the village, having a house at some distance.

In this village there lived a poor widow, who had one little son. She had been the wife of a soldier, killed in battle. This widow feared God, and it was her wish to live long enough to bring up her little son in the same holy way; but it pleased God to order it otherwise; for when little James was only three years of age, his mother was taken ill, and died in a few days, leaving her little boy a helpless orphan.

The body of the poor woman was kept to be buried till Sunday, when the clergyman always attended; and the poor little orphan never left the side of the coffin till it was put into the grave and covered with earth.

After the funeral, before the poor people left the churchyard, they consulted with each other what was to be done with the child: "For the poor baby," they said, "must not be left in need. He has lost his own parents, and we must now all be parents to him." Several of the poor people offered to take him and provide for him to the best of their power: others said, "We are all poor; it is not therefore fit that the whole charge of him should be laid on any one family: let us each do something for him, according to our means, and, with God's blessing, he will do very well."

This advice pleased all, and each person began to say what he or she would do for him.

"I," said Mary Burns, "will give him a house-room."

"And I," said Meggy Macnight, "will spin him a coat every year."

"And I," added Sandy Roberts, "will make his shoes."

"And he shall have his porridge from me," said another.

"And his buttermilk and cakes from me," said another.

"And I," said another, "will wash and mend his clothes."

So one undertook one thing and one another, and the poor people seemed comforted and pleased to think that they had organised such good care for the fatherless child. So they called little James to them, and all returned to their own homes, except one little old woman called Martha, who remained crying by the side of the grave.

This woman was a widow, and lived in a very little hut at the end of the village. She was very poor and scarcely earned enough to keep herself alive by spinning; for she was old and infirm, and her eyesight was becoming very dim. This poor widow sat by the grave and looking upon it she said, "This poor woman now she cannot hear me speak or see that I am crying over her little one! But what can I do for her little child? I can do nothing."

The poor old woman then wiped her eyes with her blue apron, and falling on her knees on the fresh turf, "O Lord God," she said, "I now lift up my prayer to thee, in the name of thy Son, who died for me upon the cross, and I earnestly beseech thee, in that name, that thou wilt teach me, by thy Holy Spirit, how I may be useful to the poor child whose mother's grave is now before me. But forgive me, O Lord," she added, "if I do wrong in making this prayer: thy will in every way, not mine, be done."

The old woman, having finished her prayer, sat down again by the grave, and began to consider what she could do for the child.

"I cannot read," she said. "nor have I any books; but I know many chapters of the Bible, and many texts of the book. Perhaps I can teach these chapters to this little one? - they may comfort and profit him hereafter."

Then she thought of the words of the apostle, which he spoke to the man who sat at the Beautiful Gate of the temple, - Silver and gold have I none, but such as I have give I thee (Acts 3:6).

Then was the old woman very much encouraged when she found that there was a way in which she might be useful to the orphan boy, and she believed that her prayer had been already heard. So she arose and left the grave, being full of sweet and joyful thoughts.

Now it happened that Mary Burns' cottage,

where the little boy was to lodge, was only a few steps from Martha's hut; and Mary Burns was always ready to do any kindness to old Martha, who, in spite of her very great poverty, was much honoured in the village.

So when Martha told Mary Burns that she wished the little orphan might come to her hut for an hour or two every day, the request was attended to.

Little James came that very evening, and sat on a three-legged stool in the chimney corner, while Martha taught him an easy verse and explained it to him. His little heart was full of his mummy, and he asked old Martha where she was gone, and when he should see her again. And this gave the good old woman an opportunity to tell him of heaven, and about the Lord Jesus Christ, through whose grace alone sinners, such as we all are, can be received into heaven.

Old Martha wished that she had some little thing that she could give the little boy in order to win his affections, and to attract him to her hut; but, without any help of this sort, God so blessed her efforts to gain his love, that, before

47

he went away, he put his arms round her neck and kissed her, and promised her that he would come again.

Before Martha lay down in her bed that night she thanked God for having so blessed the beginning of her efforts to help little James, and earnestly asked him to continue his blessing upon all her little attempts to do him good.

The next morning James appeared again, bringing with him a jug of buttermilk and some cakes which had been given to him, and saying that he had come to stay all day with her, and to hear more stories. So she taught him another verse, and told him stories about such things as she hoped would profit him.

He continued to come many days, and she taught him many texts, and even whole chapters, repeating them to him while she was spinning. She taught him also, to say his prayers, to hate a lie, and to know where to ask for help to do well, even from the Spirit of God.

It was very pleasant to see old Martha and little James sitting together in the long winter evenings, when the wind was whistling round the hut, and the snow and sleet beating against it; for in that northern country it is extremely cold. They were very happy on such occasions, which Martha improved by teaching James to knit and to wind thread, as well as to repeat many chapters.

As James grew older, he was employed during the daytime in doing work out of doors; sometimes in keeping a few sheep and goats, belonging to the village, on the sides of the hill; sometimes in driving away the birds from the gardens or cornfields; sometimes in helping to plough; and sometimes in harvest work; but he spent all his evenings with Martha, whom he called his grandmother.

In this manner the time passed away till James was eleven years old, at which period a very rich gentleman travelling that way, and taking a great fancy to James, who was a fine looking boy, offered to take him to London, and to make his fortune.

When this offer was made for the poor boy, some of his friends in the village were for accepting it, and others were against it; but Martha and Mary Burns, who loved him best, quite disapproved of it.

"London, I have heard," said Martha, "is a place of great trial for young people; and we know not," said she, "whether this great gentleman is a man who fears God or not, and will consider the soul of the poor child. And though James might become a rich man by going to London, yet, what is a man profited, if he shall gain the whole world, and lose his own soul?" (Matthew 16:26).

In this manner the good old woman talked with her neighbours; but as there were more persons in the village who were for James's going to London than for his being kept at home, Martha's advice was not taken, and the child was put into the hands of the gentleman, to be taken to London.

The parting between Martha and James was a very bitter one. When he came to take leave of her, she shut her door, and they knelt down to prayer together. She earnestly prayed that God would be with him wherever he went, and that whatever might happen to him in this world, he might hereafter be a partaker of the benefits of the death of Christ.

Soon after little James was gone, poor

Martha, who was very old was seized with an illness of which she died. Her death was an exceedingly happy one, as she placed all her trust in the Lord Jesus Christ.

And now I must tell you what became of James. It was several days before he left off mourning after his grandmother and the dear cottages in which he had been brought up; but by the time he got to London he was more cheerful. His master bought him a new suit of clothes, a hat with a silver band, very smart shoes and stockings, and some white neck-cloths; putting him under the care of his other servants, that he might be taught to wait at table; his master also permitted him to receive instruction in reading and writing.

Now James lived in a large kitchen with many servants, and I am sorry to say that he heard many bad words, and learned to drink strong drink, and to do many things which were not right. He seemed sometimes indeed very merry, and talked very fast, and you would have thought him very happy; but this was not the case for he could not bear his own thoughts - he knew that he was doing wrong. He thought much of old

Martha, and he often cried bitterly when he was alone, saying, "O that I had never left my dear home! I was happy then: my God was with me." But by degrees he got to be more careless of sin, and was more and more led astray by his own evil heart; for the Bible tells us that the heart of every man is desperately wicked.

As he grew older he was employed to go behind the carriage when his master and mistress went out; and one night, while waiting at the door of a house where there was a great entertainment, a dreadful quarrel arose among the servants. From angry words they came to blows, till at length, in the heat of anger, James was thrown by another servant with his head against a stone step, where he lay for so long a time without moving, that everybody feared he was dead. He was then taken up and carried to a hospital, where sick people are well cared for, and was laid upon a bed till a doctor could be called.

When the doctor saw him, he found that he was not indeed dead; and after he had been cared for he eventually recovered his senses. But his head was so much hurt by the dreadful fall, that his eyesight was quite gone; and he was in other ways so much injured that he never arose again from the bed on which he had been laid, although it was some months before he died.

Every attention was shown him in the hospital which could be expected; nevertheless poor James had not one kind friend to talk to him, nor to read to him, nor to speak comfort to his mind.

He lay from day to day on his bed with his eyes closed, and scarcely speaking to anyone. For some time his thoughts were all wild and confused, and he did not attempt to pray; but after a while he began to call upon his God in his grief; and his almighty Father, who through all this afflicted scene had the tenderest thoughts towards him, began to open his mind to a sense of his own unworthiness. He was made to feel, by the power of the Holy Spirit, that he had been a sinner, and that not only in the latter part of his life, when he had fallen into gross wickedness, but even in his childhood: he saw that, even in those best days, he had done those things which he ought not to have done, and left undone those things which he ought to have done, and that an evil heart had been ever leading him away from his God.

When the Holy Spirit of God, by his searching influence, had made poor James aware of his sins and of his need of a Saviour, then was comfort given to him.

One morning, as he lay in his bed, his mind seemed to dwell upon the mercies of his early days and of how he did not deserve them; and he fancied that he saw his grandmother in her little hut, sitting in her armchair, looking kindly upon him, and repeating to him her favourite chapters. Everything she had said to him was brought before his memory afresh; and he thought how she had told him, again and again, that there is no salvation for sinful man but in Christ. And that striking text, which she had taught him when he was a very little child, was brought at this time with great power to his mind, - The blood of Jesus Christ cleanseth from all sin. (1 John I:7).

"O my Saviour!" cried the poor young man, "and may I hope that thou wilt have pity on me, that thou wilt pardon me, and that thy precious blood will be effectual for my salvation? I come to thee, a miserable sinner, utterly vile and polluted; I lie at the foot of thy cross: have mercy, Lord, have mercy on me, a miserable sinner!"

Poor James now employed himself in calling to mind the chapters and verses which the devout old woman had taught him. And in this state his heart became soft and tender, so that he spent many days in grieving for his sins and calling upon his Saviour, and thanking God for having provided him, in the days of his youth, with such a friend as good old Martha, who, though she had neither food nor clothing to give him, had been enabled to teach him that good word of God, without the knowledge of which he would now have assuredly perished.

At the end of five months from the time that he was taken to the hospital poor James died. But his death was a happy one, because he had a lively faith in the death and merits of the Lord Jesus Christ, knowing himself to be a miserable sinner. And it is written, There is no condemnation to them which are in Christ Jesus (Romans 8:1).

My little children, I would have you learn from this story, that though you may not have silver and gold to give away, yet it is in your power to teach the word of God to those who know it not: you may thereby perform a far better work than that of merely giving clothes to the naked and bread to the hungry.

The May-Bee

There is a certain little village in the north of this country, where a number of small black and white cottages, surrounded with gardens, are scattered over a beautiful heath. Here are also many elms and oaks, which in the summer season afford a pleasant shade to the little flocks which feed upon the heath.

The best house in this village is the parsonage, which is placed in the churchyard. The church itself is a neat old building, with a fine tower, in which the rooks have built their nests for many years.

In this village lived little Harry. This poor little boy had lost his father and mother before he could speak, when he was put under the care of an old woman who, having a little cottage and orchard of her own, maintained herself by selling fruit and vegetables, and feeding pigs.

This old woman did not treat little Harry well;

she was very ignorant, and had not even so much as a Bible in her house; she took no care of his soul, neither sending him to church nor putting him to school; so that he remained ignorant of his God and of his Saviour.

It happened one Sunday morning in the fair month of May, while the cuckoo was singing in the woods, and the bees were gathering their sweet food from flower to flower in the cottage gardens, that the old woman, after making little Harry sweep the kitchen and feed the pigs, gave him leave to go out and play where he pleased till dinner-time. For, as I before said, she neither went to church herself, nor sent the little boy there; and, indeed, little Harry's clothes were such as she would have been ashamed to see in the church, since there was scarcely a whole thread about him.

Harry therefore set off to play, not heeding the bells of the church, which sounded melodiously from the old tower, inviting all Christians within hearing of them, from the hills and the valleys, to come forth and serve the Lord.

So little Harry ran through the garden and the orchard in which the cottage stood. Once he had climbed over the stile, he passed into a shady green lane on the other side. And while thinking what he should do, he saw before him a neighbour's boy, called William, climbing up the hedge and looking for something among the bushes.

"What are you doing there, William?" said little Harry.

"Doing?" said William, "why, I am looking for humbuzzes. Here is one that I have knocked down with my hat, and he has fallen into the bushes; so I am trying to pick him out – and now I have got him I'll make him smart for giving me so much trouble."

"Why, what will you do with him?" said little Harry,

"Look you here," said William, jumping down from the hedge, "I shall spin him on this pin."

So the wicked boy took a crooked pin out of his pocket, tied to a long piece of thread; when, thrusting the crooked pin through the tail of the harmless insect, and taking hold of the end of the string, he whirled the poor creature round in the air.

"There," said he, "see how he spins! And

listen! What a buzzing he makes! Come Harry, fetch a pin and a bit of thread, and we'll catch another for you to spin."

By the time Harry got back with his pin, William had caught another May-bee, or humbuzz (for so that insect is called in different places), which he found feeding quietly on a green leaf: so he taught Harry how to put the pin through his tail and spin him.

And thus these two naughty boys went down the lane, spinning the poor little May-bees. On reaching the bottom they saw someone coming towards them over the fields; and William called to Harry, who was a little behind, "Here comes the parson! He has been to see old John Smith, who is sick, and if he catches us with these humbuzzes, he will be sure to give it us. So hurry and hide yours. I have put mine, string and all, into my pocket."

Little Harry, having no pocket in his tattered jacket, put his hand with the May-bee in it under his ragged pinafore. But he looked so very red and confused, that when the good clergyman came up close to them, it was easy for him to see, by little Harry's face, that he had been doing some mischief, which he wanted to conceal.

"My little boys," said the clergyman as he drew near to them, "you are wandering about this Sabbath morning, with your backs turned upon the church, though the bells are ringing for divine service. And I fear," added he, "that you are engaged in some mischief, besides that of breaking the Sabbath by playing in the lanes, when you ought to be going to church."

The clergyman then looked very earnestly at each of the little boys; and observing that Harry's hand was under his pinafore, and William's in his pocket, he made them show what it was that they wished so much to hide. This good clergyman then took the poor insects, and disengaging them from the pins, he placed them gently on the palm of his hand, while he reproved the naughty boys very severely for their cruelty.

"Look," said he, "at these pretty creatures, which you have been thus cruelly tormenting: see what a fine brown polished coat they have on their backs, and how beautifully their breasts are coloured with white and black. See also what a delicate soft down covers their throats, and how bright and black their eyes appear. These little creatures are made by a Divine hand; and you have no more right to put them to pain than a giant would have to seize and to torture you." He then said to the little boys, "How should you like me now to take out my penknife and thrust it through your hand?"

And he told them that those children who take delight in tormenting living creatures of any kind are evil as is the devil. "You have often heard the devil spoken of, I doubt not," he said, "though you never come to church: because it is a common custom for people, who do not love God, to talk of the devil, and to jest with his name: but it will be no sport to such people," added he, "when they come to die, and really find themselves in his power. It is the sole pleasure of the devil to cause anguish and distress. He first tempts men and women and children to become wicked, and forsake their God; after which, having them completely under his dominion, he derides and torments them without pity.

"It was to save us from this our dreadful

enemy that the Lord Jesus Christ came down from heaven, and bore in his own body the punishment of our sins upon the cross; and you must try to become like him, for he was tender-hearted and full of pity.

"If you will come with me," continued the good clergyman, "I will receive you into my Sunday school. For there is a schoolroom near my house which is open every Sunday for the use of poor little boys. And I am sure that you will find a Sunday spent in learning the word of God more pleasant and more profitable than one wasted in idle and wicked play."

The good clergyman then took the little insects, out of which he had drawn the crooked pins, and placed them on the branch of a tree, so high that no little boy could reach them; where he hoped they might recover from their cruel treatment they had met with.

Now while this good clergyman was employed in putting the little May-bees out of danger, William jumped over a stile and ran away. But little Harry stood still; and when the clergyman had finished his work of pity, Harry went up close to him, and said, "Sir, if you will be so kind as to take me to your school, I will go with you, and learn to be good."

The clergyman was much pleased with the child's simple address; so, taking little Harry by the hand, he led him immediately towards the churchyard. And it would have pleased you very much to hear how this holy man talked to little Harry as they walked along together. First he spoke to him about the Lord Jesus Christ, and told him how much our blessed Redeemer loves little children, then he talked to him about heaven, where they who have loved our Lord Jesus Christ in this life go to live forever with him after death, and thus he continued talking to him till they reached the schoolhouse in the churchyard, where a number of little boys were at that time learning to read the holy book of God.

Mr John Law, the clerk of the parish, was the schoolmaster; but the good clergyman visited the school every Sunday, and often distributed rewards among those who tried to do well.

Then was little Harry brought to the master; who, finding on examination that he had never yet learned his letters, gave him A, B, C, printed on a card, and caused him to stand in a class with some other little boys who were also learning their A, B, C. So little Harry obeyed his directions, and worked hard at his lesson till it was time to go to church; when all the boys walked two and two to the house of God.

Observing that little Harry was ashamed of his ragged clothes, the master encouraged him by saying that God would not look at his clothes, but at his heart; telling him also that he must ask the Lord to give him a clean heart for his dear Son's sake, and not to think for a moment about his clothes.

So little Harry went to church, and behaved very quietly through the whole service; though he was so ignorant as hardly to understand anything that the good clergyman said.

When the service was over, little Harry returned home to dinner; after which he came to school again, and was taken a second time to church; from there he was brought back again to school with the other boys. And God gave him grace to behave properly at school (for no little boy can do well without God's help). There he studied so hard that he learned six letters and a little part of the Lord's Prayer.

The clergyman was very pleased to hear this. Now I must tell you that the good clergyman had neither father nor mother, wife nor children; but he had a faithful housekeeper, named Mrs Harris. And it was the custom of this good woman to come into the school every Sunday evening, and invite the best boy to drink tea with her in her neat kitchen. So this evening she came in as usual; and speaking to the schoolmaster, she said, "Well Mr Law, I am come again, as you see, to invite my company. My kettle is boiling, my tea-things are on the table, and my bread and butter is cut. Tell me, who is the best boy today? Which of all these am I to invite?"

"Why," said John Law, "if I must speak the truth, I think little Harry, who came to school this morning for the first time, has done as well or better than any other boy in the school. But yet I fear that the poor child is scarcely fit to drink tea in your neat kitchen, Mrs Harris, on account of his very shabby clothes."

"Never mind his dress, Mr. Law," said Mrs Harris; "if he wishes to be a good boy, I shall not think about his coat."

Upon this she called for little Harry; when

taking him by the hand , she led him out of the school, and brought him into her master's kitchen, where the tea-table was indeed neatly set out, and such a plate of bread and butter prepared as little Harry had not often seen.

Now Mrs Harris talked very lovingly to little Harry while they were drinking tea together; for Mrs Harris was a very pious woman, and loved her Saviour. She felt also great compassion for little Harry, showing him much tenderness, and saying everything she could think of to persuade him to be good. And among other things she told him, that although his father and mother were dead, yet if he would learn to fear and love God, the Lord Jesus Christ would take care of him, and place him with the lambs of his flock.

So when little Harry had taken as much as Mrs Harris thought proper to give him, she sent him home. But before he left her, she expressed a hope that he would come to school again the next Sunday. "And then," said she, "if you still try to do well you shall come and drink tea with me again."

So little Harry continued to attend the Sunday

school, and kind Mrs Harris invited him often to drink tea with her; for because he was an orphan, and almost utterly friendless, she really wanted to help him. She also made him shirts and socks; in addition to which her master very kindly presented him with a new hat, a suit of clothes, and a pair of shoes every year.

By these means there grew a great friendship between the housekeeper and little Harry; till one hard winter, when Mrs Harris had the rheumatism in her foot, she persuaded her master to take little Harry into the house as a footboy.

So little Harry was taken into the good clergyman's house, where he did everything he could to help Mrs Harris, who had been like a mother to him when he had hardly another friend.

The last I heard of Harry was that he was still living in the good clergyman's house, that he was becoming a very pious boy, and that having continually the fear of God before him he never did a cruel thing to any poor animal which was under his power; remembering that which is written – A righteous man regardeth the life of his beast; but the tender mercies of the wicked are cruel. (Proverbs 12:10).

My readers, perhaps, would like to hear something more of William; and I am sorry that I have nothing very pleasant to tell them concerning him. When he ran away from the good clergyman, he loitered about the fields till the bells of the church had done ringing; and all the time he kept muttering and grumbling at the good clergyman, saying he should not hinder him from spinning a humbuzz.

At length he came to a field where he saw several of these poor insects enjoying themselves in flying from tree to tree. As soon as this naughty boy discovered them, he took off his hat, and tried to knock them down; but they happily succeeded in getting beyond his reach. At last he marked one flying over his head, which he determined to bring down, but while he threw up his hat for that purpose, the poor creature made its escape to a hedge. Still, however, William was resolved to have it; so running after it up to the hedge, he was just going to catch at it, when his foot slipped, and he was thrown into the hedge, where his face was cruelly torn with the thorns. And more than this, he sprained his ankle dreadfully.

Now you, my dear little children, I beg you not to hurt any poor dumb creature; seeing that they are all the workmanship of a Divine hand, and that all of them have as keen a sense of feeling as yourselves. Remember, therefore, that he who gives them needless pain commits a grievous offence against that gracious God whose mercy is over all his works.

The Fisherman's Children

A few years ago I was visiting the north-east coast, and after preaching to old friends on the Sabbath, I wandered on the following day along the sands and among the rocks, until I was thoroughly tired; and then selecting a sheltered spot under 'the shadow of a great rock,' I sat down to rest.

Not a ripple disturbed the bosom of the great deep, which lay before me like 'a sea of glass mingled with fire.' As I mused I could not help exclaiming:

'In every object here I see
Something, my God, that points to Thee,
Firm as the rocks Thy promise stands;
Thy mercies countless as the sands;
Thy love a sea immensely wide;
Thy grace an ever-flowing tide.'

Suddenly my attention was arrested by the sound of voices chanting joyously the refrain of a hymn which I had heard, for the first time, only the previous evening. The tune was a very lively one, and the words were –

'Bright crowns – bright crowns – bright crowns,
Bright crowns – bright crowns laid on high,
For you – for me – for you – for me –
there are crowns of victory!'

Rising to my feet I proceeded in the direction of the singing and saw as I suddenly turned a corner unperceived by the singers, two young girls dabbling in a large pool of water that had been left in the hollow of the rocks by the receding tide. Sometimes they turned over the stones under which a frightened crab had taken refuge, while at others they pursued small specimens of fish that darted hither and thither with a velocity that eluded their efforts to secure them. All the time the girls kept up the refrain of the hymn and were evidently enjoying themselves, when the elder of the two caught sight of me and instantly rushed behind a projecting cliff, seizing as she ran her boots and stockings that lay upon the rocks. The younger, turning to ascertain the cause of her companion's alarm, at once recognised me, and exclaimed with a shout,

'Laws, Susie, there's now't to be freetened at; it's jist Mr. Shaw what preached last night.'

Thus assured, she came out of her hiding place, and soon we were all three seated on the rocks, engaged in a friendly chat.

The elder of the two was about thirteen years of age, while her sister would be about three years younger. They had come down to the rocks to gather 'flithers' - the local name for limpets - and had filled one of their baskets and then commenced playing, and continued their sport until my unexpected presence disturbed them. The elder was of a shy and retiring disposition and thoughtful beyond her years. The second, a girl with coal-black eyes and raven tresses, was full of fun and vivacity. Their father had perished several years before in a storm at sea, leaving them no other legacy but that of his earnest prayers and pious example. Their mother, a devout woman, had endeavoured to train them in the nurture and admonition of the Lord, sending them, as soon as they were old enough to be admitted, to our Sunday school, and taking them with her regularly to the house of God.

'And so you like singing?' I said, 'perhaps you will sing me "Bright Crowns" again, as I am wishful to learn it.'

'Susie can start it,' said the little one, 'she can sing anything. Thou knows thou can, so get on with thee;' as Susie was about to protest.

After a little hesitation the tune was struck, and the hymn sung through two or three times, after which they sang with great force and tenderness, 'Safe in the arms of Jesus.'

'And do you believe that you are safe in the arms of Jesus, and would go to be with Him if you were to die?' I asked.

For a moment both were silent; at length, Polly, the younger one, for that was her name, said, 'Susie would. She's got converted. We can't go to heaven if we are not converted, can we sir?'

'No,' I replied, 'we cannot, for as sinners we are unfit for heaven.'

'What is it to be converted?' she continued. 'Isn't it to get a new heart?'

'That is just what it is,' I answered; 'and as soon as ever we are willing to give the Lord Jesus Christ our hearts He will take them and make them clean and new.'

'But if I got a new heart, should I have to give over laughing and playing and sich like?'

'Certainly not,' I replied; 'you say your sister loves the Lord Jesus, and she was laughing and playing when I came up; you can love the Lord Jesus and be happy and joyful, while at the same time you must shun the company of all wicked boys and girls, and try to be good.'

'I think I should like to be good,' she said very softly, 'but I'm a bit young yet.'

I endeavoured to show her that many young children had found the Saviour, and after conversing with the little ones as long as I judged it prudent, parted with them and retraced my steps up the cliffs towards the town.

I had not been home long before the wind suddenly rose, and the rain poured down terrifically for two or three hours. At length the storm cleared off, and I took a walk towards the sands again. When I reached them I found the sea had become quite tempestuous, and huge breakers were rolling in upon the beach.

Presently I saw a number of fishermen attempting to launch a boat, while several women watched their proceedings with evident excitement. On enquiry, I found that my associates of the morning had not returned, and as the tide had now cut off their retreat they would have to remain for several hours unless the boatmen could get to their rescue.

As soon as I learned this, I requested to accompany them, and as there did not seem much danger, I was allowed to do so, though recommended to stay behind. Wrapped in a large pilot coat, to protect me from the wet as much as possible, I was lifted into the boat.

Again and again was she launched upon the waters, but as often driven back upon the sands by the fierce violence of the waves. At length, during a lull in the tempest, the boat was thrust through the surf, and was soon cresting the billows and on her way to the distant cliffs.

After pulling for about an hour, for the wind was dead in our teeth, we rounded the projecting cliffs, and came in sight of the objects of our search. They were standing on a piece of rock that ran out into the sea a considerable distance, and which, though above high water mark at ordinary times, was liable in such a storm as then prevailed to be swept by the huge waves breaking against it. As I was at the prow of the boat eagerly looking out, I could see them distinctly. Susie was standing calm and collected, without a sign of fear upon her countenance, though her eyes were full of sadness, the result of long and expectant waiting. In her right hand she held the basket containing the bait she had been sent to gather, while the second basket hung over her left arm, to which her sister was clinging with a frightened look, her eyes suffused with tears, and her countenance expressive of alarm.

There was considerable difficulty in reaching them; at length they were got safely on board, and the boat's head turned toward the shore, skilfully guided by an expert and practical helmsman. As we sped along, Polly lay between my knees, with her head resting upon my breast, pale as death, while her sister sat crouched at my feet, with a look of quiet rapture upon her face. I shall now pass over the landing and their reception by their widowed mother and move on to the next day for it was not until then that we learnt the girls' story.

When the rain came suddenly down, they ran to the shelter of the rocks, supposing that it was only a shower. When it was over, the flowing tide had cut off their retreat, and they had to stand and wait and watch and hope. When I asked Susie how she felt, as she saw the waves come nearer and nearer, she replied, 'Very happy; I only felt sorry for mother and Polly. I told her to trust in Jesus, for He was near us, though we could not see Him, and we sang the hymn, "Jesus, lover of my soul," until we could not sing any longer. I did not want to be drowned; but I knew if I was, that I should go to see Jesus, and be with Him forever.'

I perceived that Polly was unusually silent. She sat on one knee and nestled up to me. When I was about to take my leave she looked up wistfully and shyly into my face and whispered: 'I prayed in my heart to Jesus, when the waters were coming in upon us, and said, "Lord Jesus, give me a new heart, and make me fit to go to heaven," and I believe He has.'

Polly's subsequent history leads me to believe that her cry out of the darkness and the storm was not unheard.

Scenes on the Sea

Charles Kingsley has said that the sea is most beautiful in winter, and this, in the sense in which he used the words, is undoubtedly true. It is when the north-east wind blows with terrific fury, and the billows roll in with indescribable force, that the ocean is seen in its sublimest aspect. A poet once said,

> Dost thou love to see the rushing
> Of the tempest in its might?
> Dost though joy to see the gushing
> Of the torrent in its height?

I have witnessed such a sight again and again; and as I have watched the billows rolling 'mountains high,' and breaking with their long wild sweep for miles along the shore, we have been reminded of Bernard Barton's beautiful poem:-

'Beautiful, sublime and glorious,
Mild, majestic, foaming free;
Over time itself victorious,
Image of eternity.'

But while it may be interesting for the landsman to gaze upon the sea in such a state, let us not forget the dangers encountered by those who do business upon the great waters, and the anxiety felt by their friends.

It has been my lot to witness some of the most furious storms with which the east coast has been visited and to share with the inhabitants their anxiety for their brave bread-winners.

One storm burst upon us with alarming suddenness. The fishermen had gone off to sea a little before daylight, and were pursuing their work as usual, when a hurricane arose, and swept over them with a terrible fury. Again there was a general flocking to the cliff-top and sands by excited crowds, who watched with anxiety the appearance of the boats as one after another came in sight. Now we beheld them tossed upon the summit of a mountainous wave, and again apparently engulfed in the devouring sea.

'He's gone!' one would exclaim when some boat was out of sight a moment longer than usual; while the next instant another would shout, 'There he is!' as the struggling craft bravely rose, as if by miracle, out of the yawning deep.

These scenes continued for several hours, during which all the vessels save five safely reached the beach, and the men were safely landed amid the shouts of some and the tears of others. Four of the missing boats had taken refuge at Flamborough, while the fifth, with broken rudder, rode out the gale partially sheltered by the stony Brig.

During the same storm the crew of a Flamborough coble were picked up by a sailing vessel, and afterwards landed at a southern port. At Scarborough, all the boats were not so favoured, for while several of them escaped without serious damage, one coble was overturned and three of her men perished each of whom left a family to mourn his loss. On the same day a schooner was blown completely over, and three of her crew perished within sight of the pier; the captain and a boy managed to scramble upon the bottom of the vessel, and were ultimately rescued by a passing ship.

Walking the next morning upon the beach, I discovered that a beautiful vessel had been driven upon the rocks and become a total wreck. Her crew had escaped with their lives but had lost everything else. I could not but feel sad as I saw spars and timbers floating about, the solitary remnants of what, but a few hours before, had been a noble structure. And so, I thought, it is with many a promising youth and lovely maid.

While musing on the blasted hopes and ruined reputations of many I had known, I was reminded of the poem by Professor Upham:

I saw a wreck upon the ocean flood,
How sad and desolate, no man was there;
No living thing was on it, there it stood;
Its sails all gone;
Its masts were standing bare;
Tossed in the wide, the boundless,
howling sea;
The very sea-birds screamed
and passed it by.

And as I looked the ocean seemed to be
a sign and figure of eternity.
The wreck an emblem seemed
of those that sail
without the pilot, Jesus, on its tide.
Thus, thought I,
When the final storms prevail,
shall rope, and sail, and mast
be scattered wide;
And they with helm and anchor lost,
be driven,
in endless exile sad,
far from the port of heaven.

On returning one night from a country appointment, I was distressed to hear that no less than seven of our yawls were missing. As each vessel carried about ten hands, some idea may be formed of the anxiety prevailing in the town. Women, whose husbands and sons were in the missing vessels, were in a state of intense anxiety and the scene at the telegraph office was really distressing. The distracted females were anxious to hear if any tidings had reached Hull or Grimsby, and it was with the utmost reluctance that the clerk informed them that as the offices in these towns were closed, he could obtain no response to his enquiries before six the next morning. Slowly and silently they retired to their homes, but not to sleep. If ever we prayed earnestly for sailors and fishermen it was that night. Next morning we were at the cliff-top before daylight, but no tidings had been received. The sea was rolling in upon the beach in dark and sullen waves, and the faces of the weather-beaten fishermen looked as gloomy as that of the ocean. Six, seven, eight o'clock arrived, and no news! At last, about nine o'clock, the news flashed across the wires, written by the trembling hand of the telegraph clerk, that six Filey yawls were safe at Grimsby, and in the Humber. This still left one unaccounted for, but about noon, she was also heard of, and a great load of anxiety was removed from many a heart.

But though all the vessels were safe, all the hands were not. One fine young fellow, the son of a personal friend of mine, was carried overboard and seen no more. His parents were devoted Christians, and had prayed for his safety, but they will see his face no more until the sea gives up the dead that are in it. Yet who shall say that their prayer was unanswered? God's ways are not our ways and He may see fit to answer our prayers not by granting the letter of our request, but by doing for us and ours far more exceeding abundantly than we asked or thought.

But the fury of that same terrible storm was felt all along the shore. Hundreds of lives were lost and numerous homes left desolate. One touching incident connected with these disasters is recorded in the Sunday Magazine for 1878, by Mrs. Charles Garnett. We give the story in full:- '"He holdeth the sea in the hollow of his hand." - And what a broad, restful, loving hand His is. I thought so as I heard the following facts. Perhaps some mother whose cry goes up to God for her young son night and morning may think so. Perhaps some weary ones telling themselves that the raging of the storm which beats about their lives is too fierce to heed the still small voice may take comfort to look upwards, and may perchance see a rift in the dark clouds driving overhead.

'A mighty storm howled along the north-east coast of England on Friday and Saturday, the 8th and 9th February 1861. The wind was blowing from east-north-east and lashed the foaming and racing waves to fury. In the bay of Hartlepool eighty-one vessels were driven ashore, forty-three of which became total wrecks, and eighty brave hearts were stilled for ever beneath the waters, and eighty desolate homes were left sailorless on shore. Groups of anxious inhabitants dotted the coast and watched the vessels tossed like corks on the waves which bore them reefwards.

'The five lifeboats which belong to the two Hartlepools were all out rescuing the crews of stranded vessels, when about ten o'clock on Saturday morning a stout vessel was seen in the offing, making for the shore. The signal of distress was flying, and she ran before the wind landwards. The spectators hoped that she would come far enough in to make rescue by the lifeboats a possibility. Her name was the Rising Sun, and the eager eyes which watched her could make out that she was severely damaged and was quite unmanageable. A long low reef called Longscar Rock lies out in the bay about a mile from shore, and could she but round this she would be in comparative safety, or at least within reach of help. On she came, rolling on the waves which bore her to destruction; each moment she neared Longscar Rock, and the watchers gave a cry as they saw her strike heavily upon its end; and in a few moments she sank, the hull disappeared, and the waters hissed and foamed about the two masts which continued to stand out of the sea. Upon these the crew, seven in number, could be counted as they clung for life. Thousands of fellow creatures by this time crowded the beach, but the Rising Sun was only one amongst the many vessels in a similar condition. All the lifeboats were engaged, and the only means left of rescuing the seven men clinging like flies to the shaking mast was the rocket apparatus, and before this could be obtained one of the masts upon which were hanging three men broke away, and they perished. The other could be still seen, and three more men and a boy were distinctly counted upon it. With intense anxiety and all possible speed the apparatus was adjusted; but just as the light touched the powder and the mortar fired the ball and line across the wreck, this last mast disappeared with its precious burden, and the grey-green waves around the reef rose and fell, unbroken by a sign of human life. Sadness fell on all faces, and many a rough hand drew itself across misty eyes, which in vain scanned the waste of the ocean. Hopelessly the line was drawn in, but as it neared the beach something was felt to be entangled in its folds. That something was the sailor-boy! At first it seemed that his young life had been beaten out of him, and sorrowful voices said, "He's quite dead." "Anyhow, let us try and bring him to." Plenty of willing hands were there to help. On the spot where he had come to land every means for his recovery was tried. Joyfully the onlookers observed in a short time faint signs of life; then he struggled and moved and ultimately became conscious.

With wild amazement he gazed on the vast crowd of kind and sympathising friends. They raised him to his feet. He looked up into the weather-beaten face of the old fisherman near him, and asked:

'Where am I?'

'Thou art here my lad.'

'Where's the captain?'

'Drowned my lad.'

'The mate then?'

'He's drowned too.'

'The crew?'

'They're all lost my lad: thou art the only one saved.'

The boy stood overwhelmed for a few moments then he raised both his hands and cried in a loud voice:

'My mother's been praying for me! My mother's been praying for me!'

And then he dropped on his knees in the wet sand and hid his sobbing face in his hands.

Hundreds heard that day this tribute to a mother's love, and to God's faithfulness in listening to a mother's prayers.

A Night on the Deep

'Now it is pleasant, on the summer eve,
When the broad shore retiring waters leave,
Awhile to walk upon the firm fair sand,
Where all is calm at sea, all still on land;
And then the ocean's produce to explore,
As floating by, or rolling on the shore.' - Crabbe.

It was just such an evening in June, 1857, when John Williamson, William Jenkinson, and William Ross, three fishermen belonging to Filey, pushed off from the shore in their little boat for the purpose of 'shooting,' that is, putting down their lines. They were brave and fearless men, who had been born close by the sea, and as their boat sped rapidly over the water, they merrily sang –

'We are out on an ocean sailing,
To a home beyond the sky;'

and other hymns which they were accustomed to sing in their religious services when on shore, until, when they had proceeded about five miles, the wind began to freshen and the surface of the sea to be agitated sufficiently to toss their boat in a manner which would have been unpleasant for a landsman. But these hardy sons of the ocean thought nothing of it. If anything it delighted rather than discomposed them, for each one of them could say with Byron:

'And I have loved thee, Ocean, and my joy
Of youthful sports was on thy breast to be
Borne like thy bubbles onward. From a boy
I wantoned with thy breakers, they to me
Were a delight; and if the fresh'ning sea
Made thee a terror, 'twas a pleasing fear,
For I was, as it were, a child of thee,
And trusted to thy billows, far and near,
And laid my hand upon thy mane,
as I do here.'

They only laughed as the boat rose and sank upon the billows. But in a moment, while they were all unconscious of danger, a sudden squall of wind caught the boat, and instantly capsized her! So unexpected was the accident, that the men, unprepared for it, were thrown into the water, Williamson and Jenkinson clear of the boat, while Ross was partly underneath her. Jenkinson soon reached her again, and laying hold of Ross, dragged him on to her bottom. Williamson also succeeded in swimming to her, and the three poor fellows found themselves together once more, but exposed to the most fearful peril.

What a condition was theirs! But let us describe the scene in the words of the only survivor, from whose lips we took down the account: -

'As soon as we got on her Williamson said, "The Lord help us." The boat was two or three feet under water, bottom upwards, but leaning partly on one side. Jenkinson handed us a bowl each to help keep us afloat. I tied him fast to one with a "tow," which I loosed off the bowl strop, took off my neckerchief and "wove" it through the bowl strop, and then he made it fast round me. Williamson had his in his hand. The wind now rose and the water dashed against us with such fury that Williamson was washed off the boat. Seeing his perilous condition, I took an oar, and pushed it towards him, and pulled him on the boat again. Then he said, "Let's all shout as hard as we can, likely there may be someone riding under the cliffs."

We shouted until we were hoarse, but no one heard us, and we gave over, thinking it was of no use. The wind continued to increase and blow more furiously. We commenced singing –

> *"Jesus, lover of my soul,*
> *Let me to Thy bosom fly,*
> *While the troubled waters roll,*
> *While the tempest still is high."*

'The boat gradually sank deeper and deeper, and the waves again washed Williamson off. I took an oar a second time to try to reach him, but with reaching too far, fell off the boat into the water, and was washed ever so far from her. I swam to her, but when I got back I found that she was so much under the water that when my feet touched her I was up to my waist. After some struggling I got hold of the end of the mast and hung there. I could see Williamson not far from the boat, but he was so exhausted that he could not reach us. Finding that he was sinking, he sang the lines :

> *"Cover my defenceless head*
> *With the shadow of Thy wing."*

'I could just see the top of his sou'wester out of the water, and a minute or two after he sank, and we saw him no more. When we were left to ourselves, Jenkinson said, "Ross, can you pray?" I said, "No, I don't know how." He said, "Then say the words after me;" and he began to pray, and I prayed also; then he sang and I sang, until I was led to believe that Jesus Christ, who died for sinners, died for me, and could save me on the bottom of a boat far out at sea. After this I felt all my fear go away, and had a feeling that I should not die.

'After a while I thought I would try to swim to shore, and left the boat, but soon failed, and got back to her with difficulty. Jenkinson was still engaged in prayer; indeed he never ceased to pray. I rested as well as I could for about five minutes, and then ventured a second time. When Jenkinson saw me leaving him, he said, "O, Lord, help me, I am left by myself." I could not bear to hear him say that, and returned, determined not to leave him any more. We both continued to sing and pray, as well as we had strength. It was getting very dark now, and the boat was sinking deeper and deeper. At length there was so much wind, and she got so deep, that we leaped off her. I could not see anything, but felt for Jenkinson, and at last found him, but his head was under water. The bowl to which he was tied had "shifted," and kept him under. I could feel his hair in my hands. While struggling to keep myself afloat, I felt a line in my hand; this I found was fast to the boat, and I hauled myself to her. I tried in vain to find Jenkinson; but it was so very dark that it was impossible to see anything. After a while the moon began to rise, and just over the white cliff. I had my eyes on the moon, and looked toward Filey, wondering if ever I should see my friends there again. Then I began to think that some boat might come to seek us, but none came. It was now about ten o'clock, and a little later a Billy -boy bound for the north came to leeward of me. I shouted as loud as I could shout; but it was of no use, no one heard me, and she passed on. She appeared to be so near that I could have thrown a stone into her if I had had firm standing. About a quarter of an hour after a schooner came to windward. Again I shouted, but could not get him to hear, and he passed on. Oh, the loneliness I felt left all by myself, with nothing but the boundless sea around me. But I was not alone, for I felt the Lord was with me, strengthening and comforting me. I lifted up my heart to Him who said, "I will never leave thee, I will never forsake thee;" and, blessed be His holy name, I did not cry in vain. A wonderful peace filled my soul, and to cheer myself I sang –

"Abide with me, fast falls the eventide;
The darkness deepens; Lord with me abide!
When other helpers fail and comforts flee,
Help of the helpless, O abide with me."

'When I had sung the hymn I found that I was drifting out to sea very fast, and could scarcely keep myself on the boat, as she could not bear my weight. To prevent her from sinking, I had to keep creeping on my hands and knees sideways upon her. After doing this for some time, I tried to take off the rudder, thinking that if she went down suddenly it would help to keep me up, but I could not get if off. I then tried to lower the sail, but failed again. I believe this was providential, as it is very likely that her sail kept her from sinking. No one can imagine what I felt. The darkness increased, and though I was wonderfully happy, feeling that the Lord had pardoned all my sins, yet I could not help wishing that some vessel might come and pick me up. Besides I was so young, and I thought of those at home; and though not afraid to die, I wanted to live. But what could I do? Nothing but what I had done before – pray, and look to the Lord for deliverance.

'After knocking about till, I should think, nearly two o'clock, I thought I saw a sail in the distance, and concluded it was a boat from Filey coming to seek us. My heart leaped for joy. Alas! Alas! I was doomed to be disappointed. I soon found out it was only the flag flying at the bowl to which I had fastened William Jenkinson. I, however, still held on to the boat, and though the wind got still higher, and blew very strong, and the waves washed over me, I never lost hope. I believed in the prayers that had been offered for me by my parents and brothers would not be in vain. But oh, how I longed for the morning! At last, day began to break, and the first thing I saw was a ship, which seemed to be steering straight for me. "Now," I thought, "I am going to be saved!" There were three other vessels coming close round Flamborough Head, and I thought again, "Well, if this one does not come to me, some of the others will be sure to reach me, for I am right in their track." But the ship came right on, and got nearer and nearer. I tried to shout, but was afraid I could not make them hear. At last I saw them lower the boat, and that lifted my heart up. Then I saw two men in her, pulling for me. Then they came up to me, laid hold of me, and took me in.

'After the men reached me, the first and only words I could say were, "Pull for yon bowl." They did so, and found Jenkinson's body still tied to it, took it in, and pulled for the ship. As soon as we got alongside, they handed me two or three pots of coffee into the boat to refresh me. After drinking the coffee, I was taken on board. This was about half-past four in the morning."

The vessel was the Shepherdess, Captain

Britlington, of Hartlepool. The captain, fancying he heard a voice, said to the men, 'Don't you hear a voice like a man's on the water?' They replied, 'It will be the birds from the cliffs come out to feed.' The captain, however, was not convinced, but thinking he again heard a distant shout, called the mate out of bed, saying, 'I fancy I hear a man's voice. Try if you can make anything out.' The mate took the glass, and, carefully scanning the surface of the water, said, 'I see something which looks like a man on a plank.' The vessel was instantly brought to bear down upon the object, and poor Ross was rescued in the manner described.

After being taken on board he was treated with the greatest kindness. 'I was in such a state,' says he, 'that they dared not let me go to bed, but kept giving me nourishing things. Though it hindered him very much, the captain said he was determined to land me at home, if possible, and bore over to the north; and at length, when off Scarborough, he succeeded in tacking, and reached Filey Bay about two o'clock that afternoon. A boat came and took me, and the body of Jenkinson, out of the ship, and landed me. I could not stand, but they placed me in a carriage and drove me to my mother's. I was very light-headed after that, and it was some days before I was myself again.

Near the area well-known as 'The Cliff Top' there was a cottage where resided William Ross's widowed mother. Many years ago her husband perished at sea, and left behind him a large family of sons most of whom were brought up to earn their bread upon the waters, as fishermen and sea-farers. The father's memory was dear to these children, for he had lived a truly pious life, and his prayers had been so far answered, that at the time of which we are writing, all the sons, with the exception of William, had been truly converted to God. When the family found that the boat had not returned, they were in great trouble. His brother John said to the writer, 'When noon arrived we had little hope of his safety. Still we could not think that the many prayers, which had been offered on his behalf, were all in vain. I remember being in my mother's when a vessel came into the bay, with a flag, flying half-mast high. I knew in a moment what that meant, and while mother was in another room, removed my brother's stockings, guernseys, and other things that were hanging upon a line, and put them out of sight, for though I was only a boy when my father was drowned, I very well remember how the sight of his clothes used afterwards to affect my dear mother; but in her losses she was perfectly resigned to the will of God.'

The news that a vessel was coming into the bay with a flag half-mast high spread with extraordinary rapidity, and speedily crowds of anxious but subdued people were gathered upon the sands. It was soon known by the relatives and friends that only one out of the three had returned alive. The body of William Jenkinson was soon landed, and buried a day or two afterwards amid the tears and lamentations of numerous spectators. The body of Williamson was found near Flamborough a few days afterwards, and interred at Filey the following day. The scene at the grave was indescribably affecting.

Williamson left a widow and four children, the eldest of whom, a fine young woman, was to have been married to William Jenkinson in a few weeks. It may be interesting to the reader to be told that, not long after, William Ross became the husband to another of Williamson's daughters and that he and his wife were known to walk before the Lord in righteousness and true holiness. The two men who perished were members of the church at Filey and when the funeral sermon was preached on the occasion of their death, at the close of it several of the companions of William Ross, who had heard of his marvellous preservation and happy conversion, gave their hearts to God.

Hundreds of Christian mariners have testified to the power of Divine grace to sustain and compose the mind in the midst of the fiercest storms, and in the immediate prospect of a watery grave. In such moments the believer finds that

'Faith pierces the gloom
and dispels his fears,
For a vision of bliss to his soul appears,
Of the haven of rest, that peaceful lies
In the home of his heart, beyond the skies.'

The Foolhardy Captain

'Shall you anchor off the point, captain?' asked a passenger.

'I mean to be in dock on the morning tide,' was the captain's brief reply.

'I thought, perhaps, you would telegraph for a pilot,' returned the passenger.

'I am my own pilot, sir;' and the captain whistled contemptuously.

'He's in one of his daring moods, and I'll bet anything you like that he takes the narrow channel,' remarked a sailor quietly, as he passed us to execute some order.

'Is it dangerous?' asked the same passenger uneasily. 'Very, in a gale; and there's one coming, or I'm no sailor,' replied the man: 'but if any man can do it, it's himself. Only he might boast once too often, you know.'

Evening came and the gale was becoming what the sailors called pretty stiff, when the mate touched my arm, rousing me from a pleasant dream, in which smiling welcomes home held prominent place.

'We are going in by the narrow channel, sir,' said he; 'and, with this wind increasing, we may be dashed to pieces on the sand-bank. It is foolhardiness, to say the least. Cannot you passengers compel him to take the safer course?'

I felt alarmed, and hastily communicated with two or three gentlemen; and proceeding together to the captain, we respectfully urged our wishes, and promised to take the responsibility for any delay that this change in course would result in.

But, as I anticipated, he was immovable. 'We shall be in dock tomorrow morning gentlemen,' said he. 'There is no danger whatever. Go to sleep as usual, and I'll engage to awake you with a land salute.' Then he laughed at our cowardice, took offence at our enquiries, and, finally swore that he would do as he chose; that his life was as valuable as ours, and he would not be dictated to by a set of cowardly landsmen.

We retired, but not to rest; and in half-an-hour the mate again approached us saying, 'We are in for it now; and if the gale increases we shall have work to do that we did not expect.'

Night advanced, cold and cheerless. The few who were apprehensive of danger remained on deck, holding on by the ropes to keep ourselves form being washed overboard. The captain came up, equipped for night-duty; and his hoarse shout in the issue of commands was with difficulty heard in the wild confusion of the elements; but he stood calm and self-possessed, sometimes sneering at our folly, and apparently enjoying himself extremely, surrounded by flapping sails, straining timbers, and the ceaseless roar of winds and waves. And we endeavoured to take courage from his fearless demeanour. But presently there arose a cry of 'Breakers ahead!' The captain flew to the wheel; the sails were struck, but the winds had the mastery now, and the captain found a will that could defy his own.

'Boats made ready!' was the next hurried cry; but, as too often occurs in the moment of danger, the ropes and chains were so entangled, that some delay followed the attempt to lower them; and in the meantime, we were hurrying to destruction. The passengers from below came rushing on deck in terror, amidst crashing masts and entangled rigging, and then came the horrific shock, which gave warning that we had touched the bank; and the next was the fatal plunge that struck the foreship deep into the sand, and left us to be shattered there at the wild waves' pleasure.

It is needless to dwell upon the terrors of that fearful night. I was among the few who contrived to manage the only boat which survived; and scarcely had I landed with the morning light, surrounded by bodies of the dead and fragments of the wreck, borne up by the rising tide, ere I recognised the body of our wilful, self-confident captain.

He was like one of those who, on the voyage of life, refuse counsel and despise instruction; who practically recognise no will but their own; who are wise in their own conceits, and satisfied with their own judgement, and trust in their own hearts, and if left to be filled with their own ways, must make frightful shipwreck just when they suppose themselves sure of port.

'Peace, peace, to those far and near,'

says the Lord.

'And I will heal them.'

But the wicked are like the tossing

sea, which cannot rest,

whose waves cast up mire and mud.

'There is no peace,' says my God,

'for the wicked.'

Isaiah 57:19-21

'You will again have compassion on us;

you will tread our sins underfoot

and hurl all our iniquities into

the depths of the sea.'

Micah 7:19

'If any of you lacks wisdom he should ask of God, who gives generously to all without finding fault, and it will be given to him. But when he asks, he must believe and not doubt, because he who doubts is like a wave of the sea, blown and tossed by the wind. That man should not think that he will receive anything from the Lord; he is a double-minded man, unstable in all he does.' James 1: 5-8

'The men were amazed and asked, "What kind of man is this? Even the winds and the waves obey him!"'

Matthew 8:27

'There were those who went

out to sea in ships;

they were merchants on the mighty waters.

They saw the works of the Lord,

his wonderful deeds in the deep.

For he spoke and stirred up a tempest

that lifted high the waves.

They mounted up to the heavens

and went down to the depths;

in their peril their courage melted away.

They reeled and staggered like drunken men;

they were at their wits' end.

Then they cried out to the Lord

in their trouble,

and he brought them out of their distress.

He stilled the storm to a whisper;

the waves of the sea were hushed.

They were glad when it grew calm,

and he guided them to their desired haven.

Let them give thanks to the Lord

for his unfailing love

and his wonderful deeds for men.

Let them exalt him

in the assembly of the people

and praise him in the council of the elders.

***

Whoever is wise let him heed these things

and consider the great love of the Lord.'

Psalm 107: 23-32; 43

Mary Martha Sherwood

The story of 'Joseph and his Brethren' has been regarded as one of the most beautiful stories in the Bible; and many think that it presents an excellent picture of virtue, devotion and forgiveness for young and old to immitate.

Mrs Sherwood, in the tale of 'The Little Woodman,' especially desired to lead young people to think of Divine mercy and protection, and to inspire the hearts of her readers to forgiveness. These were the qualities of a Christian nature that she tries to depict in all her narratives.

Mary Martha Sherwood was born in the small village of Stanford-on-Teme, Worcestershire on 6th May 1775. The daughter of a clergyman, she became one of the most prolific writers of her day. A very lively, pretty girl, she was sent away to school in Reading. The Abbey school that she went to was in fact the same school that Jane Austen and her sister Cassandra had previously attended.

In 1797 she met her cousin Henry Sherwood who had been in France during the revolution, and had even been imprisoned and then shipwrecked. They fell in love and eventually married. By the time she and her family returned from India in 1816 Mary had five children of her own and three adopted orphans as well as a large collection of novels to her name.

Mary Sherwood was an acquaintance of Elizabeth Fry, the prison reformer, and once joined in her inspection of Worcester gaol.

Her writing continued and during a period of eight years she had published over eighty books for young children (some of which were translated into Hindu).

George Shaw

It is believed that George Shaw was a minister based in and around the coastal area of Yorkshire moving from Filey to Grimsby and other fishing communities towards the middle or end of the 19th century.

Today the communities of Filey and the Yorkshire fishing villages and towns still have a strong Christian presence through churches and mission halls.

There are missioners and societies who still make it their business to reach out to those men who make their living from the sea. Though technology and safety procedures today mean that this job is safer than it once was, fishermen still live a very dangerous and hard life on the sea.

When reading these stories of the men and their families who trusted in the Lord for their salvation all these years ago please pray for those people working in the fishing indsutry today, that they too will experience God's protection and saving power.

Other Classic Fiction Titles

Little Faith
A little girl learns to trust
O.F. Walton
Faith, persecuted by her grandmother when her
mother dies, finds faith and justice.
ISBN: 1 85792 567X

Christie's Old Organ
A little boy's journey to find a home of his own
O.F. Walton
Christie is a street child. He sets out with Treffy, the
Organ Grinder, to find a place of peace.
ISBN: 1 85792 5238

A Peep Behind the Scenes
A little girl's journey of discovery
O.F. Walton
Rosalie is forced from place to place with her brutal
father's travelling theatre - if only she could find a
real loving relationship?
ISBN: 1 85792 5246

Saved at Sea
A young boy and a dramatic rescue
O.F. Walton

Alec lives with his gandfather in a lighthouse. A little girl is rescued from a shipwreck and changes all their lives.

ISBN: 1-85792-7958

Sunshine Country
A young boy finds a bible and his real family
Kristiny Royovej

When Pablo was little he was found wandering in the forest. Now he is being looked after by a kind hearted old grandfather who has adopted him as his own. But lots of things happen when Pablo discovers the Bible in the secret cave and a new woodcutter arrives in the village.

ISBN: 1-85792-855-5

A Basket of Flowers
A young girl's fight against injustice
Christoph von Schmid

Falsely accused of theft, thrown from her home, her father dead - Mary learns to trust God.

Exciting tale with a dramatic twist.

ISBN: 1 85792 5254

Other Classic

Stories

Mary Jones and her Bible
The story of a girl whose inspirational desire to have
a Bible in her own language led to the founding of
the National Bible Society.
ISBN: 1-85792-5688

Chilhood's Years
An excellent collection of short stories including the
fascinating myster, 'The Bible in the Wall.'
ISBN: 1 85792-7133

Children's Stories D L Moody
Stories used by this world famous evangelist to
teach Christian truths within his own Sunday school.
ISBN: 1 85792-6404

Children's Stories J C Ryyle
Stories for children by this great communicator
including the well known classic, 'The Two Bears.'
ISBN: 1 85792-6390

Classic

Devotions

The Peep of Day
A popular devotional title from the 19th century.
Written by F. L. Mortimer to be used
within a family setting.
ISBN: 1-85792-5858

Line Upon Line 1
The second in the F.L. Mortimer's devotional titles.
Covers scripture from Genesis, Exodus, Numbers
and Joshua.
ISBN: 1 85792-5866

Line Upon Line 2
The third in the classic devotional series by F. L.
Mortimer. This titles covers 1 and 2 Samuel; 1 and 2
Kings; Daniel and Ezra.
ISBN: 1 85792-5912

***

Look out for the our new edition of the devotional
title: Morning Bells and Evening Thoughts
by Frances Ridley Havergal

LIGHTKEEPERS
Start collecting this series now!

Ten boys who changed the world
David Livingstone, Billy Graham, Brother Andrew,
John Newton, William Carey, George Müller, Nicky
Cruz, Eric Liddell, Luis Palau, Adoniram Judson.
1-85792-5793

Ten boys who made a difference
Augustine, Hus, Luther, Zwingli, Tyndale, Latimer,
Calvin, Knox, Shaftesbury, Chalmers.
1-85792-7753

Ten boys who made history
C H Spurgeon, Jonathan Edwards, Samuel
Rutherford, D L Moody, Martin Lloyd Jones, A W
Tozer, John Owen, Robert Murray McCheyne, Billy
Sunday, George Whitfield. 1-85792-8369

Ten girls who changed the world
Corrie Ten Boom, Mary Slessor, Joni Eareckson
Tada, Isobel Kuhn, Amy Carmichael,
Elizabeth Fry, Evelyn Brand, Gladys Aylward,
Catherine Booth, Jackie Pullinger   1-85792-6498

Ten girls who made a difference
Monica of Thagaste, Catherine Luther, Susanna
Wesley, Ann Judson, Maria Taylor, Susannah
Spurgeon, Bethan Lloyd-Jones, Edith Schaeffer,
Sabina Wurmbrand, Ruth Bell Graham.
1-85792-7761

Ten girls who made history
Ida Scudder, Betty Green, Jeanette Li,
Mary Jane Kinnaird, Bessie Adams, Emma Dryer,
Lottie Moon, Florence Nightingale, Heanrietta
Mears, Elisabeth Elliot.
1-85792-8377

Other Trailblazers

CHRISTIAN FOCUS

Staying faithful – Reaching out!

Christian Focus Publications publishes books for adults and children under its three main imprints: Christian Focus, Mentor and Christian Heritage. Our books reflect that God's word is reliable and Jesus is the way to know him, and live forever with him.

Our children's publication list includes a Sunday school curriculum that covers pre-school to early teens; puzzle and activity books. We also publish personal and family devotional titles, biographies and inspirational stories that children will love.

If you are looking for quality Bible teaching for children then we have an excellent range of Bible story and age specific theological books.

From pre-school to teenage fiction, we have it covered!

Find us at our web page:
www.christianfocus.com